This book is for:

_____

The Very Best Grandmother in the Universe

according to me:

_____

4012334

To Beverly Elaine Fischman Steinberg, the bestest
"Baba Baila" in the universe—DJS

For Grandma Rhin and my lovely mum, Sharon—
the two most wonderful grandmas I know—RH

GROSSET & DUNLAP
An imprint of Penguin Random House LLC, New York

First published in the United States of America by Grosset & Dunlap,
an imprint of Penguin Random House LLC, New York, 2022

Text copyright © 2022 by D. J. Steinberg
Illustrations copyright © 2022 by Ruth Hammond

Library of Congress Cataloging-in-Publication Data is available.

Manufactured in China

ISBN 9780593387139

10 9 8 7 6 5 4 3 2 1 HH

MY GRANDMA
IS THE
BEST!

BY
D. J. STEINBERG

ILLUSTRATED BY
RUTH HAMMOND

GROSSET & DUNLAP

Kisses Bank

Grandma and Grandpa, you're finally here!
I missed you forever—it's true!
And while we were waiting to see you this year,
I've been saving up all of my kisses for you!

Too Much Art!

My grandma keeps our art
on her refrigerator door.
It's filled from top to bottom—
there's no room for any more.
Now what will Grandma do?
I suppose sooner or later,
she's going to have to get herself
another 'frigerator!

The Universe in Grandma's Purse

Need a tissue? A toothpick?
Some hand sanitizer?
A cough drop? A breath mint?
Some shades or a visor?
Whatever you need in the whole universe,
just go ask Grandma—it's there in her purse!

Checkers Champ

I beat my grandma at checkers today!
I jump-jump-jumped all her pieces away.
My grandma must be awfully proud
that she taught me how to play!

A New Do!

Granny—come sit in this chair.
It's time to schmancy up your hair.
Take out the ribbons, clips, and ties.
Now ready, set . . . open your eyes!

Puzzle On!

My grandma dumps the pieces out.
We sort them bit by bit.
We spread them 'cross the table
where my grandma likes to sit.
It may take us forever,
but we'll never ever quit
'cause piece by piece, we puzzle on
till all the pieces fit!

World's Greatest Babysitter

Mom and Dad, don't pick me up—
I'm having too much fun.
I'm still babysitting Grandma,
so I'll call you when I'm done!

Star of the Stage

How could that be my grandma?
That little girl singing onstage . . .
I wish I could jump in the photo
and meet her when she was my age!

Talent show – 1960

The Doctor Is In

Grandma, it's time to give you your shot.
Now be a brave girl for me.
I'm a very good doctor—this won't hurt a lot.
Hold your arm out and . . . one, two, three!

Catch of the Day

Oma picked me up at dawn
to go down to the bay.
We cast our lines and told each other
stories the whole day.
And we didn't catch a single fish,
but I caught something better . . .
a day with Oma to myself—
just her and me together!

Ring-a-Ling!

Make way, people . . . *Ring-a-ling!*
We're going for a ride—
Grandma in front, my sister in back,
and me on my bike by their side!

Nana's Lap

My favorite place in the whole wide world
is here on Nana's lap.
She reads me a book or two or nine
until ZZZZZZZZ . . . I drift off for a nap.

THE WORRIED
LION

SPACE!

UNICORN

JUMP!
ABC

ALL ABOUT
CATS

My Greatest Cheerleader

My grandma always tells me,
"There's nothing you can't do!"
And just the way she says it,
I believe it, too!

Names for Nanas

What do you call your grandmother . . .
Nana or *Grammy* or *MayMay*?
Bubbe, *Oma*, or *Tutu*?
Abuela, *Safta*, or *Nai Nai*?
No matter how you say it,
and no matter what their name . . .

. . . all grandmas round the world
love their grandkids just the same!